Fear factor

YIKES!

SCARIEST
STUNTS EVER!

By Jesse Leon McCann

SCHOLASTIC INC.

New York   Toronto   London   Auckland   Sydney

Mexico City   New Delhi   Hong Kong   Buenos Aires

*For Stewart Lovelace,
confidant and friend*

Photo Credits: 11 & 41: maze illustrations by SI Artists; 19: © Susan Goldman/Bloomberg News/Landov; 26: © Hulton-Deutsch Collection/CORBIS; 65: © Photodisc via SODA

Pages 14, 28–29, 31, 38, 44–45, and 62–64, content used with permission from NBC.com

ISBN 0-439-80348-9

Fear Factor TM & © 2006 Endemol Netherlands B.V.

Published by Scholastic Inc.
SCHOLASTIC and associated logos are trademarks
and/or registered trademarks of Scholastic Inc.

12 11 10 9 8 7 6 5 4 3 2 1   6 7 8 9 10/0

Printed in the U.S.A.
First printing, January 2006
Designed by Michelle Martinez Design, Inc.

Introduction

The Danger Factor

Since its premiere five years ago, *Fear Factor* has become a phenomenon seen all over the world. Besides the weekly version of the show, you can see it almost every night in syndication. You can watch it on DVD, play the video game, and experience the *Fear Factor Live Show* at Universal Studios.

As you probably know, *Fear Factor* challengers have to endure highly dangerous stunts, not once but twice, in almost every episode— those gut-wrenching, spine-tingling, high-in-the-air, fast-moving, glass-breaking, truck-jumping, trapped-underwater, touch-and-go stunts!

In this book, we'll describe some of the jaw-dropping competitions in detail, and even rate them with our *Fear Factor* **Yikes-O-Meter**— one star ★ being a little scary, five stars ★★★★★ being heart-wrenchingly terrifying!

But there's a whole lot more in this book! Interviews with contestants from the show, exciting puzzles, fearsome stunt records, terrifying trivia and quizzes, and pictures of *Fear Factor* contestants in action! We'll also talk about different phobias. Phobias are persistent fears that freak some people out. We'll list some of the more interesting phobias—like phobophobia, which is the fear of phobias!

So, on with the show!

But before we do—this important warning:

The stunts from *Fear Factor* described in this book were designed and supervised by trained professionals. They are **extremely dangerous** and should not be attempted . . . by anyone . . . anywhere . . . **anytime!**

Jesse Leon McCann
Los Angeles, January 2006

RISKY RECORDS!

STATS FOR SOME SERIOUSLY SCARY *FEAR FACTOR* STUNTS

- You're suspended high in the air (And by "high" we don't mean standing on your kitchen counter. No, think way higher. WAY, WAY higher.) and you've got to jump from platform to platform to transfer flags to your partner. "No big deal," you're thinking? Well, try it when the platforms are moving farther and farther apart. Now, are your feet shaking a little more in your boots? A record-breaking couple team was able to transfer 19 *Fear Factor* flags. **YIKES-O-METER RATING: ★★★★**

- Two trucks, traveling single-file, a beam between them. Got the picture? You've got to release a *Fear Factor* flag by crossing halfway across the beam, on foot. Then you have to cross back again. Next up is riding a bike across the entire beam from one truck to the other. And, hey, the beam is thin—so leave the training wheels at home. The quickest time in *Fear Factor* history: 13.7 seconds. **YIKES-O-METER RATING: ★★★★★**

- Anyone up for a swim? First, here's the stunt: A rope is suspended horizontally from one helicopter to another, dotted with *Fear Factor* flags. The goal is to release all the flags by moving across the rope, then drop into the water below, where your tired, worn-out arms now have to swim to a buoy several yards away. Record time: 1 minute, 41.3 seconds. **YIKES-O-METER RATING:** ★★★

- Two speedboats racing across a lake, side by side . . . and the contestants have to transfer six *Fear Factor* flags from one boat to the other. Record time in *Fear Factor* history: 2 minutes, 7 seconds (two players tied with the same time!) **YIKES-O-METER RATING:** ★★★★

PERILOUS PUZZLER!

SOLVE THIS HIGH-OCTANE *FEAR FACTOR* CROSSWORD:

ACROSS

7. It means "unsafe"; rhymes with "stranger bus."

11. Players often have to crawl through this; in real life, it is built so we can drive through a mountain.

12. To get out of a trap, sometimes contestants need one; you use this to unlock your front door.

13. Challengers had to hang on to the wing of one as it flew faster than 100 miles per hour.

14. The contestant who wins at *Fear Factor* is the _____.

DOWN

1. Players had to ride one of these two-wheelers across a thin rail between two moving trucks.

2. An October holiday celebrated on *Fear Factor* is _____.

3. Used in many *Fear Factor* stunts, this is sometimes called a whirlybird or chopper.

4. Many *Fear Factor* contestants had to do stunts atop one of these; rhymes with "skill king."

5. Contestants are often asked to complete a stunt while submerged in _____.

6. You get lots of _____ if you win a *Fear Factor* episode.

8. Players often have to gather up as many of these as they can during a stunt.

9. Sometimes *Fear Factor* players are bound with these devices made with many steel links.

10. In many stunts, contestants have to climb up these; you might have to do this in gym class.

Answers on page 72

TERRIFYING
TRIVIA QUIZ!

CAN YOU MATCH THE CORRECT SYMPTOM WITH ITS PHOBIA?

Q: Acrophobia is the fear of what?
a. crossing the street
b. apple crops
c. crows
d. heights

Answer: d, Heights, so don't look down!

Q: If your friend has claustrophobia, he's afraid of what?
a. Santa Claus
b. confined spaces
c. animal claws
d. sharp knives

Answer: b, Confined spaces, so never, ever let him get trapped in a closet!

Q: What is the phobia name for fear of electricity?
a. zappophobia
b. electrophobia
c. plugophobia
d. buzzophobia

Answer: b, Yes, electrophobia is its shocking name!

ThE PhOBiC Facts File

PTEROMERHANOPHOBIA IS THE FEAR OF FLYING!

Zooming through the sky at tremendous rates of speed. Or hovering far above a crystal-clear lake with only the birds for company. What could be more . . . *terrifying*?! If you're one of the people who have pteromerhanophobia, the fear of flying, these activities don't sound like much fun. (I'm betting that the *Fear Factor* stunt of traveling on a rope between two helicopters didn't sound like much fun either!) But don't feel alone—lots of people have the same fear. In fact, many celebrities would rather keep their feet firmly planted on the ground—such as actor Billy Bob Thornton, science-fiction writer Ray Bradbury, and pop singer Javine, just to name a few!

By the way, two other names for the fear of flying are aviotophobia and aerophobia.

ON *FEAR FACTOR*, CONTESTANTS HAVE TO LEAVE ANY FEAR OF FLYING ON THE GROUND!

A FEARSOME PUZZLE
TO AMAZE YOU!

You're in a *Fear Factor* helicopter, then—*splash!*—you dive into the ice-cold water of a lake. You hop onto the Jet Ski waiting for you there. The contest begins when the clock starts! Can you capture three *Fear Factor* flags by circling them with your pencil—and make it to the pier to stop the clock—in under three minutes? Get a clock or a timer, and a trusty pencil . . . then GO!

(Hint: Instead of writing in this book, make photocopies of the page. Then solve the maze puzzle on the copies with your friends. You and your pals can compete to see who's the fastest Fear Factor *challenger!)*

IT'S A GREAT LAKE RACE!

Maze solution on page 72

DID YOU KNOW DID YOU KNOWOW ? .

- The first airplane, invented by the Wright Brothers, stayed in the air only 12 seconds during its maiden voyage on December 17, 1903. *Hardly enough time for the flight attendants to serve peanuts, or—in* Fear Factor *style—worms!*

- Another name for a tightrope walker is a "funambulist." *Do you think that's because it's "fun," or maybe because it's a good idea to keep an "ambulance" close by?*

- Balance depends mostly on the way liquid moves around in the three canals of the inner ear. *Hmmm . . . We wonder what happens when you're, say, diving into a wedding cake made entirely of creepy, crawly bugs and they get into your ears? What? We couldn't hear you. . . . What??*

- According to some statistics, the most dangerous job in the United States is that of a sanitation worker. *There's more than one reason the job stinks!*

- The National Institute of Mental Health says the most common fear is of public speaking. *That doesn't seem to be Joe Rogan's fear!*

MATCH THE
FEAR FACTOR WORDS!

**DRAW A LINE FROM THE WORD IN THE FIRST
COLUMN TO THE WORD IN THE SECOND
COLUMN THAT MOST CLOSELY MATCHES.**

1. Hazard

2. Elimination

3. Detonation

4. Automobile

5. Tumble

6. Race

7. Champion

8. Extreme

9. Transfer

10. Crash

11. Structure

12. Blunder

a. Fall

b. Dash

c. Shift

d. Excessive

e. Dismissal

f. Building

g. Explosion

h. Mistake

i. Danger

j. Winner

k. Impact

l. Vehicle

Answers on page 73

✔ ASKED & ANSWERED!

WE ASKED ACTUAL *FEAR FACTOR* CONTESTANTS ABOUT THE MOST DARING AND DANGEROUS THING THEY'D EVER DONE! HERE'S WHAT THEY SAID:

- ✔ "I got locked on a rooftop and had to jump to a fire escape!"
- ✔ "I went to Spain with my college friends and, believe it or not, I ran with the bulls!"
- ✔ "I rode my mountain bike from Chicago to San Diego. I dipped my front tire in Lake Michigan and my back tire in the Pacific. The trip took my best friend and me a month and a half!"
- ✔ "I climbed down a rock face sixty feet high that my friends and I secured ourselves. We didn't know what was down there!"
- ✔ "Cliff diving off ledges into lakes . . . who knows what you're gonna hit?"
- ✔ "Penning cows . . . We had a herd of eighty cows, and we had to round them up in a little pen. Let's just say they weren't very happy, so they would kick and buck and I had to be in there with them!"
- ✔ "Went skydiving on my twenty-seventh birthday!"
- ✔ "I jumped off a bungee tower, then at the apex of rebound, I unhooked and free-fell sixty feet into an airbag!"

SOME WISE QUOTES
FROM PEOPLE OF WISDOM!

"The most dangerous strategy is to jump a chasm in two leaps."
—Benjamin Disraeli

"Take calculated risks. That is quite different from being rash."
—General George S. Patton

"It's a dangerous business going out your front door."
—J. R. R. Tolkien

"I believe that one of life's greatest risks is never daring to risk."
— Oprah Winfrey

"If you're never scared or embarrassed or hurt, it means you never take any chances."
—Julia Sorel

"I am not afraid of storms, for I am learning how to sail my ship."
—Louisa May Alcott

"Courage is doing what you're afraid to do. There can be no courage unless you're scared."
—Eddie Rickenbacker

"Obstacles are those frightful things you see when you take your eyes off the goal."
—Hannah Moore

"Don't be afraid to see what you see."
—President Ronald Reagan

"One of the greatest discoveries a man makes, one of his great surprises, is to find he can do what he was afraid he couldn't do."
—Henry Ford

ANOTHER HEART-POUNDING CROSSWORD!

SOLVE THIS HAZARDOUS PUZZLE:

ACROSS

4. Players had to climb down and up a ladder below one as it floated above the Pacific Ocean; rhymes with "shrimp."

9. On *Fear Factor*, players have been flung out of these; they sound like they involve felines, but they don't.

10. Contestants drove really fast up one to get their cars flying far through the air.

11. Contestants flipped their cars as an _____ went off under them; it's loud and fiery.

12. To win many of the *Fear Factor* challenges, you have to have a good sense of _____.

14. Big, heavy, round thing used to knock down buildings; on *Fear Factor*, players became human versions of one; rhymes with "trekking Paul." (2 words)

DOWN

1. Players have to do this to get from one platform to another; it means "leap."

2. Quite often, *Fear Factor* challengers have to collect these during a stunt.

3. One of the best shows on TV! (2 words)

5. On an early episode of *Fear Factor*, contestants were dragged behind a _____; it's something seen in many western movies and rhymes with "cage roach."

6. Like acrobats do under the circus big top, players had to jump and grab one of these, as they hung high in the air; rhymes with "nap please."

7. This goes very fast on the water.

8. Challengers are often lifted high into the air by a _____; it's used at construction sites.

13. If you fall, you hope one is below to catch you.

Answers on page 74

CAN YOU ANSWER THESE
FEARSOME PHOBIA QUESTIONS?

DON'T BE AFRAID! GO AHEAD AND TRY!

Q: What is the fear of heights called?
- a. fallophobia
- b. cliffophobia
- c. altophobia
- d. vertiphobia

Answer: c. If you got that right, you're highly intelligent!

Q: The fear of pain is called what?
- a. algophobia
- b. ouchophobia
- c. acheaphobia
- d. suffophobia

Answer: a. Algophobes really hate needles!

Q: What is bathmophobia the fear of?
- a. taking a bath
- b. the Batmobile
- c. depths
- d. Bath, England

Answer: c. That's right, they always watch their steps!

DID YOU KNOW ... ?

- Producers of *Fear Factor* originally considered naming the show *Scared Stiff*, among other things. *The name* Fear Factor *definitely has more of a punch!*

- During the Tesla Coil stunt, contestants had to wear a special chain mail suit to protect them from the lightning arcs—the Tesla Coil used in this stunt is 2000 times more powerful than an electric chair. *Intense high-voltage shocks? Okay, yeah, now I see where they got the "Scared Stiff" thing from!*

- In the Electric Maze stunt, the metal handcuffs used in the stunt acted as a conductor, ensuring that each time a contestant was shocked, the partner would also feel it. *Man, talk about partnership. That really takes "Till death do us part" to a whole other shocking level!*

- Every physical *Fear Factor* stunt is tested many times for safety reasons by the coordinating producer and crew. *That's why they get paid the BIG bucks!*

- Some *Fear Factor* stunts are filmed on location at Universal Studios. *Some of those roller coaster rides must seem like a walk in the park after the terrifying* Fear Factor *stunts!*

ThE PhOBiC Facts File

MOTORPHOBIA IS THE FEAR OF AUTOMOBILES!

In their engines, automobiles carry lead-acid batteries, which contain hazardous materials, including approximately eighteen pounds of lead and a gallon of sulfuric acid. Statistics suggest that you're safer in an airplane than a car. (Tell that to the folks afraid of flying!) So, you can see why it's not completely unreasonable for motorphobes to fear autos. But you might want to keep this to yourself—or your parents may never let you get your learner's permit!

By the way, the fear of speed is called tachophobia.

A *FEAR FACTOR* CONTESTANT ONCE DROVE HIS AUTOMOBILE UP A RAMP, DID A 360° FLIP, AND LANDED THE CAR BACK ON ITS WHEELS! AWESOME!

TOP TEN

Fear factor
SCARIEST STUNTS!

We got together a group of folks and asked them which stunts really made their hair rise and their hearts race with fear. Here are their top picks. And while it's not a list that's set in stone (after all, many of *Fear Factor*'s scariest stunts are undoubtedly still to come), it is a pretty dangerous list! You can bet that each of these stunts rates a full **five stars** on *Fear Factor*'s **YIKES-O-METER.**

10. Underwater Hallway ★★★★★

In a large water tank, contestants were submerged in icy water—so cold, they were given wet suits to avoid hypothermia (this is when your body temperature goes way below normal and it is very dangerous). In the tank was a fifty-foot-long Plexiglas "hallway." The underwater hallway was divided into three locked chambers, each containing *Fear Factor* flags. Once underwater and inside the hallway, with the cold water all around them and pressing down on their lungs, players used a key attached to their wrists to move from one chamber to the next. The goal was to collect as many flags as possible (without passing out, of course!). Several air pockets were available along the way, if needed. But the stunt was based on speed, so you can bet that contestants stopped to take a precious breath only when they absolutely needed it!

9. Flatbed to Flatbed ★★★★★

Picture sitting in an automobile on top of a semitrailer flatbed, while facing the road. Attached to the flatbed is a second flatbed, coated with oil. Ready to slip, slide, and glide? When the players in this stunt received the green light, they had to hit the gas and jump the car from the first flatbed to the second. But wait, it gets better. While doing this jump, the semitrailer sped and swerved along a desolate highway! Those players whose cars did not clear the gap between the two flatbeds, or skidded off the second flatbed, were disqualified. *Ouch! Better luck next time, slowpokes!*

8. Inverted Helicopter ★★★★★

Chop! Chop! Time is a tickin'. In this head-rushing stunt, players had to hang upside down by their ankles from the bottom of a helicopter. The helicopter hovered above the icy, choppy water of a lake. Attached to a chain near their ankles were three keys, one of which unlocked their chained leg. A release cord was attached near their other leg. Players had to find the correct key to free their chained ankle (Where's Harry Houdini when you need him?), then pull the release cord to free their second ankle, to plunge down into the water far below.

7. Dog Attack ★★★★★

Dogs can smell your fear. So we hope the contestants in this stunt either stayed calm or loaded up on the deordorant! At the California Sheriff's Training Facility in San Bernardino, players wore padded protective gear and faced a bunch of ferocious dogs. They had to make their way through a maze while locating six flags and then raise them by hitting a nearby lever. Around every corner was a different breed of attack dog that had been trained specifically to stop strangers. These weren't your fluffy, froufrou dogs either. We're talkin' saliva-dripping, fearless canines. Lots of sharp teeth and ripped padding during this stunt!

6. Burning Building ★★★★★

Ever dream of being a firefighter? You have to have guts to face those fiery flames. Turn up the heat and get a load of this stunt! At a fire-training tower used by the Santa Fe Springs, California, Fire Department, players suited up in heavy firefighter uniforms with oxygen tanks. The tower was then lit and quickly engulfed in flames—burning upward of 2,000°F! *(Whew! Can somebody get me some water?)* Once the players climbed up a long truck ladder to the fourth floor of the tower and entered the fiery building, the clock started ticking. First things first, they had to locate the fire hose in the scorching heat, and then follow it to the fire's location. After putting out the blaze, each player had to brave the thick, dark smoke to locate a rescue dummy. With the smoke making it extremely difficult to breathe, they had to drag the dummy up and out to safety. Once the dummy landed in a rescue basket, the players' final times were calculated.

5. Boat Jump ★★★★★

As two speedboats sped alongside each other at speeds topping forty miles per hour, players had to jump from one boat to the other. It was all in the timing because the distance between the two boats constantly changed, so they had to time their jumps perfectly. It didn't go quite so perfectly for some players. More than one unlucky contestant slammed into the other boat—face first! *Ouch! Does anybody have the number for a good plastic surgeon?*

4. Airplane Walk ★★★★★

A red vintage biplane traveled at speeds up to 100 miles per hour. The "lucky" contestants had to travel in the cockpit of the plane. When the plane reached a soaring altitude of 4,000 feet, the fearless players had to climb out onto a wing, retrieve a flag, and get back into the cockpit!

3. Extreme Building Plunge ★★★★★

Anyone up for a little fall? In this off-the-wall stunt, each player was dangled from the top of a 65-story building and then dropped. *Rewind—did you say 65 stories?* Yup, you read that right, 65 stories! That alone is scary enough to freak most people out! But the game must go on! As the players fell along the glass exterior of the structure, getting closer and closer to the hard pavement, they grabbed as many flags as possible. Those who got the most flags moved on. And those who didn't get flags were probably just happy to be alive!

2. Walking the Plank ★★★★★

Ahoy, mateys! This stunt took place on a large schooner, similar to what pirates used to sail. Contestants had to walk the plank, just like prisoners were forced to do in the old pirate days! Each player was shackled with a heavy ball and chain, and then tipped over a wooden plank into the unforgiving ocean. While underneath the sea holding their breath, they had to unscrew the shackles as fast as they could, swim to the surface, and touch the ship to stop the clock! *Yar!*

1. The Mother of All Stunts ★★★★★

The one you've been waiting for—the one to make your spine tingle with fear! This was a couples challenge, and each pair of players began the stunt in the back of a speedboat. As the boat raced through the harbor, the couples had to climb a hanging ladder to pull themselves into a helicopter that was hovering above the choppy water. The helicopter then whisked each couple back over solid ground, so they could jump onto a moving semi! No rest for the weary! Then couples had to climb inside the trailer, where a car was waiting for them. After putting on safety gear, the pairs got into the car, revved it up, and crashed out of the trailer and onto the pavement behind the truck to stop the timer. *Wow! The winners should consider a career in action movies!*

DANGER–RELATED FEAR FACTOR WORD SEARCH!

FIND THE WORDS ON THE LIST BELOW AND CIRCLE THEM!

(Hint: Some words might be backward or diagonal!)

ACROBAT	PLATFORM
ADVENTURE	RACE
BULLDOZERS	STRENGTH
COMPETE	STUNT
FALLING	SWIMSUIT
KNOWLEDGE	TREASURE
NAVIGATE	UNDERWATER

Answers on page 74

W	G	Y	E	T	E	P	M	O	C	C	K	K
K	K	R	N	T	B	F	R	M	S	P	H	H
Y	T	A	S	G	A	J	L	W	K	T	M	M
S	A	C	T	T	T	G	I	K	G	K	J	R
R	B	E	Y	K	U	M	I	N	K	P	E	O
E	O	Q	L	L	S	N	E	V	F	T	M	F
Z	R	G	B	U	X	R	T	K	A	K	Q	T
O	C	R	I	K	T	K	J	W	H	N	B	A
D	A	T	V	S	G	T	R	R	R	N	F	L
L	P	K	A	D	V	E	N	T	U	R	E	P
L	N	D	C	H	D	F	A	L	L	I	N	G
U	H	W	Q	N	E	R	U	S	A	E	R	T
B	G	T	U	K	N	O	W	L	E	D	G	E

ThE PhOBiC Facts File

ENTOMOPHOBIA IS THE FEAR OF INSECTS!

Were you ever lying in bed and felt like something was crawling over your skin? You whipped off the sheets, looked down, but didn't see anything? After convincing yourself that everything was fine, you settled yourself back down—only to feel that same creepy, crawly feeling again! If you're out at a picnic and are freaked out by little bugs and ants (and if you take the old saying "Don't let the bedbugs bite" to heart) then you might have entomophobia. Consider yourself bugged out, and a word of advice—don't apply to be a contestant on *Fear Factor* (we tend to like bugs here)!

By the way, the fear of ants is myrmecophobia.

PEOPLE WITH *ENTOMOPHOBIA* WOULDN'T LIKE BEING ON *FEAR FACTOR*—PLAYERS HAVE HAD TO JUMP INTO TANKS OF INSECTS, AND EVEN DRINK INSECT SLUSHIES!

DID YOU KNOW . . . ?

- In early Europe, there was a popular superstition that if you wore turquoise, you could never suffer a broken bone—instead, the turquoise itself would shatter and thus prevent the accident.
Get some turquoise to the Fear Factor *set, stat!*

- Pain from any injury or illness is always registered by the brain, yet the brain itself can't actually "feel" pain.
That's a real head-scratcher!

- The first person to go over Niagra Falls was Annie Edson-Taylor. She plunged over the side and thrashed about inside of a wooden barrel and lived to tell the tale.
Yeah, but she really didn't get to see much of the scenery.

- When he was a boy, inventor Thomas Edison suffered a permanent hearing loss following a head injury. One of his ears was actually pulled roughly while being lifted

aboard a moving train. *Which leads one to wonder . . . was Thomas already cooking up* Fear Factor *stunts back then?*

FEAR FACTOR
CONTESTANTS INTERVIEWED

FROM UNDERWATER RELAYS TO BARREL BALANCING—WITH A WHOLE LOT OF LEECHES IN BETWEEN—BEST FRIENDS AMBER AND TABITHA STUCK TOGETHER AND WON THE GAME!

FEAR FACTOR: **What stunt was the most challenging for you and why?**

AMBER: The hardest challenge for me was getting through the first stunt. I was under the cold water for close to five minutes and the hardest part for me was just not quitting.

TABITHA: The last stunt because I am scared of heights and I was shaking. But I knew it was Amber's strength, so it worked out okay.

FEAR FACTOR: **Did you have any phobias going into the competition?**

AMBER: The only phobia I had was rats, but the good thing was that I did not have to face rats on the show.

TABITHA: No, not any phobias. I hate rats, but looking back, I could have done anything I was faced with.

FEAR FACTOR: Other than winning, what was the best part about your *Fear Factor* experience?

AMBER: Being able to travel to California. I had never been on the West Coast. I also loved the *Fear Factor* crew; everyone showed us a good time.

TABITHA: Getting closer to my best friend, whom I didn't think it was possible to get any closer to! We had the best time getting away together, away from our routine. *Fear Factor* is a bonding experience.

FEAR FACTOR: What will you do with the $50,000?

AMBER: It is going in the bank. I am a single mother of a one-year-old, and I won it for her.

TABITHA: Nothing other than save it. I am taking a thousand dollars to go on a shopping spree but other than that I am saving it. Maybe it will be a down payment on a house one day.

FEAR FACTOR: Did having a partner help you?

AMBER: Yes, very much so. Whenever my confidence was questioned, she pulled me through it. My strengths were her weaknesses, and her weaknesses were my strengths.

TABITHA: Yes. Her strengths were my weaknesses, and her weaknesses were my strengths. We pulled each other through.

ANOTHER ROUGH-EDGED, HARD-PLAYING FEAR FACTOR WORD MATCH!

DRAW A LINE FROM THE WORD IN THE FIRST COLUMN TO THE WORD IN THE SECOND COLUMN THAT MOST CLOSELY MATCHES.

1. Steer	a. Truck
2. Conceal	b. Foe
3. Strange	c. Struggle
4. Effort	d. Prize
5. Opposition	e. Tired
6. Rugged	f. Fans
7. Weary	g. Navigate
8. Search	h. Hide
9. Audience	i. Catch
10. Trap	j. Hunt
11. Semitrailer	k. Tough
12. Reward	l. Mysterious

Answers on page 75

A ONE-ON-ONE CONVERSATION WITH A *FEAR FACTOR* CHAMP!

FEAR FACTOR: As everyone kept failing the first stunt, did you think you'd be able to do it?

DWAYNE: I have to admit that seeing everyone else fail was kind of discouraging. However, I just focused on my objective.

FEAR FACTOR: What was being trapped in that body bag and plunged into the water like?

DWAYNE: Oh, man! It was outrageous! It was hard to see anything, because the plastic compressed against my face as soon as I was plunged into the freezing water. I felt like a frozen chicken in a Ziploc freezer bag being thawed out in cold water. From now on, I won't be freezing chickens anymore!

FEAR FACTOR: You made it look so easy! What was your strategy?

DWAYNE: My strategy was to stay calm, not panic, and try to feel for the keyhole to unlock the handcuffs as the bag was equalizing.

FEAR FACTOR: Any big plans for the total cash winnings of $50K?

DWAYNE: Of course! I plan to pay off my two vehicles and invest wisely for my family's future.

ThE PhOBiC Facts File

KAKORRHAPHIOPHOBIA IS THE FEAR OF FAILURE OR DEFEAT!

President Abraham Lincoln once said that he considered his Gettysburg Address "a flat failure." Not so, when many consider it one of the greatest speeches in history. Lincoln was wrong—he didn't fail. On the other hand, when contestants fail on *Fear Factor*, there's no doubt about it—they lose! It's eat-crow, hide-their-faces, take-a-hike-down-the-walk-of-shame time for them. So, you can understand why they might be sore losers. They probably had to gulp down some disgusting all-you-can-eat buffet, or dangle from a helicopter, and still walk away with nothing. Tough blow—we'd be embarrassed, too!

By the way, the fear of ridicule is katagelophobia.

PEOPLE WITH *KAKORRHAPHIOPHOBIA* MIGHT NOT ATTEMPT *FEAR FACTOR* OR ANY OTHER CONTEST—THEY'D BE AFRAID OF SNEERS AND JEERS IF THEY LOST!

SEE HOW YOU SCORE ON THIS
TRIVIA QUIZ!

Q: How high is the tallest cliff that anyone's ever jumped off of with a parachute, which is called BASE jumping?
- a. 19,300 feet
- b. 2,000 feet
- c. 800 feet
- d. 500 feet

Answer: a. Which gave the jumpers lots of time to think about what they'd do if the parachute didn't open!

Q: What is the fastest anyone has ever ridden a bicycle?
- a. 55 miles per hour
- b. 70 miles per hour
- c. 102 miles per hour
- d. 167 miles per hour

Answer: d. Bet the rider could deliver a lot of newspapers going that fast!

Q: What is the longest skateboard rail grind?
- a. 17 feet 10 inches
- b. 21 feet 2 inches
- c. 36 feet 9 inches
- d. 56 feet 1 inch

Answer: c. We'd sure like to see the library with a handrail that long!

CROSSWORD CRAZINESS CONTINUES!

SOLVE ANOTHER THRILL-PACKED *FEAR FACTOR* PUZZLE:

ACROSS

1. What challengers often do while in cars on *Fear Factor*; rhymes with "smash."

5. Method sometimes used on *Fear Factor* to see who goes first; rhymes with "join Ross."(2 words)

6. You have to apply these to stop a car.

7. Another name for racetrack; players raced at the one in Irwindale, California; rhymes with "bead tray."

10. It means you've made up your mind to win when you have_____; rhymes with "concentration."

11. When two or more contestants try to get to a place first, it's called a _____; rhymes with "face."

DOWN

1. A jolly December holiday celebrated on *Fear Factor*.

2. What players make when they fall into the water.

3. Increments of time that players win by; also, what it's called when you're having another helping of yummy *Fear Factor* squid pie!

4. When you're heels over head, as *Fear Factor* contestants sometimes are! (hyphenated word) (opposite of rightside-up)

6. Take a deep one if you're swimming underwater.

8. It's like a motorcycle for riding on water; rhymes with "pet bee." (2 words)

9. Where boats are kept when not in use; rhymes with "barber."

Answers on page 75

- Once, while filming a bull-riding stunt, twenty bulls got loose and stampeded toward the *Fear Factor* crew. *Was it a planned stampede? Maybe these bulls had had enough!*

- *Fear Factor Live* at Universal Studios is the first time a reality television show has been turned into a theme park attraction. *Not hard to believe, because it's the BEST reality show out there!*

- *Fear Factor* casting staff start out with 1,000 hopefuls per episode and whittle them down to between six and twelve contestants who actually appear on the show. *Some people get turned down, then push their fears aside and apply again—and if lucky, are chosen!*

- According to *Fear Factor* producers, the odds are more in your favor for getting into Harvard than being chosen to appear on *Fear Factor*. *Yeah, but defying the odds is what* Fear Factor *is all about!*

- It takes a crew of more than 150 people to put each episode of *Fear Factor* together. *Which would you rather do—move heavy Plexiglas around all day, or wrangle scorpions? These folks earn their pay!*

STARTLING STATISTICS!

MORE DIRELY DANGEROUS
FEAR FACTOR RECORDS

- The most flags collected in three minutes from the wing of a jet plane as it rocked back and forth, high in the air: 15 *Fear Factor* flags.

YIKES-O-METER RATING: ★★★★

- Players had to climb out one side of a helicopter as it hovered twenty-five feet above a lake. Then they had to travel underneath it, hugging the helicopter for dear life, while using a cargo net fastened to the runners. When they finally reached the other side, they had to pull themselves back inside the door on the other side. Best record: 40 seconds.

YIKES-O-METER RATING: ★★★★

- The longest time a player could stay on a real-live, rip-snortin' angry, 2,000-pound bull: 7 seconds.

YIKES-O-METER RATING: ★★★★★

- The most flags collected as players balanced themselves on top of a bus while it whipped around, swerving crazily back and forth over a Hollywood set: 12 *Fear Factor* flags.

YIKES-O-METER RATING: ★★★

- The longest distance traveled, when competitors had to speed a car up a fiery ramp engulfed in flames, flip the car over, and somehow land it in a pile of boxes: 62 feet, 7 inches.

YIKES-O-METER RATING: ★★★★

✓ ASKED & ANSWERED!

WE ASKED PLAYERS WHAT STUNT WAS THE MOST CHALLENGING FOR THEM, AND WHY? HERE'S WHAT THEY SAID:

✔ "The airplane stunt, by far. I didn't know you would need so much strength against the wind, and I am not the strongest person in the world!"

✔ "The very first bicycle stunt was challenging because I had not been on a bike in twelve to fifteen years!"

✔ "I'd have to say the most challenging stunt as far as difficulty goes would have to be the flaming crossbow/witch's brew, because it was impossible to see the target once the flame was lit."

✔ "The underwater stunt, because I am really afraid of drowning!"

✔ "Honestly, the tram stunt when we were hanging on the ropes over the water, the first stunt. That was the hardest, not because we were up high (I blocked that out), but because you can't control when your muscles are going to give out on you. It was pure strength. You needed good coordination, but if you were heavy and had no upper body strength there was no way you were going to last, especially with the wind and the swaying tram."

✔ "The last stunt, the water stunt. The pressure inside the cylinder and at the bottom of the pool was so intense. I felt like my ear-drums and lungs were bruised for a few days, but luckily in the moment I was focused on winning and I got paid!"

✔ "For me, it was the last stunt, because I was so high in the air and the wind was blowing. I was scared I would fall but I didn't. I was crying on the inside!"

COURAGE CORNER!

FEAR WAS NOT A FACTOR
FOR THESE BRAVE FOLKS

WIM HOF OF THE NETHERLANDS has the record for the longest time spent in direct, full-body contact with ice, at 1 hour, 8 minutes. *No, Wim, your mom said girls like "nice" guys, not "iced" guys!*

ALEXANDER GRAHAM BELL didn't just have a knack for inventing telephones. He set a world water speed record of 70 miles per hour in a hydroplane (those awesome boats that lift out of the water as the speed increases) he designed when he was seventy-two years old. *With the years a tickin'—he just kept on kickin'!*

PAUL CRAKE OF AUSTRALIA holds the record for running up the 1,576 steps of New York City's Empire State Building in 9 minutes 37 seconds during the "2001 Empire State Run-up." *Somebody had their power breakfast! (Or maybe he had entomophobia and was imagining being chased up the stairs by millions of bugs!)*

A. J. HACKETT OF NEW ZEALAND dropped 590 feet, 10 inches off of the Sky Tower Casino, the highest building in Auckland, New Zealand. All right, calm down, he didn't just "drop off," he was bungee jumping! His fall ended just 40 feet from the concrete pavement before he rebounded. *Lucky thing, too, because that would have definitely left a mark!*

ANOTHER MAZE—
WILL IT FAZE YOU?!

You're high above the city, and the people far below you look like ants! You have to ride a bicycle over the thinnest of rails to compete in this contest. Can you crush your fears and do it? The challenge begins when the clock starts! Capture three *Fear Factor* flags by circling them with your pencil, and make it to the elevator to stop the clock in under three minutes and you'll be a *Fear Factor* champ! Get a clock or a timer, and a trusty pencil. Ready? Set? *GO!*

(Hint: Instead of writing in this book, make photocopies of the page. Then solve the maze puzzle on the copies with your friends. You and your pals can compete to see who's the fastest Fear Factor *challenger!)*

A RACE HIGH IN THE SKY—
NOT FOR THE DANGER-SHY!

Maze solution on page 76

DAREDEVIL TALES OF DERRING-DO, OR HAREBRAINED STUNTS WE DO NOT DARE?
YOU DECIDE!

On July 2, 1982, Larry Walters, a 33-year-old Los Angeles truck driver who'd never piloted a plane or balloon, tied 45 weather balloons to his lawn chair and took off! Luckily, he was wearing a parachute. Moments after takeoff, Larry was 16,000 feet in the air! Passing jetliner pilots didn't know what to think, and Larry was so amazed by the view, he forgot to take pictures with a camera he'd brought along. When Larry got tired of the view, he used a pellet gun to pop some of the balloons so his strange "air" craft could float back down to Earth. He almost landed without a hitch, except for those pesky power lines. He got himself a little tangled up in the electric lines. *(Ouch, Zap!)* But where he really got into trouble was with the police who were waiting down below for him. They arrested Larry for his crazy stunt!

The most famous modern daredevil is Evel Knievel. He has thrilled millions with his death-defying motorcycle jumps through fires, over rows of cars, and even over a tank of hungry sharks. He holds the record for having the most bones broken. In January of 1969, the world watched in awe when he successfully jumped the enormous fountains at Caesar's Palace in Las Vegas, only to crash on the other side and end up in a coma for weeks with a shattered pelvis, fractured hip, and smashed right femur. Surgeons rebuilt his leg with a two-foot-long, three-inch-wide piece of steel. *(Good luck going through the metal detectors at the airport!)* On May 31, 1975, a record crowd of over 90,000 at Wembley Stadium in London, England, watched as Evel crashed upon landing, breaking his pelvis after clearing thirteen double-decker buses, one of the last great jumps of his career. Evel once said, "Fear is high-octane fuel for success. You have got to know how to handle it, how to harness it. If you risk your life, you have got to have fear."

ThE PhOBiC Facts FiLE

TAUROPHOBIA IS THE FEAR OF BULLS!

The producers of *Fear Factor* have cited the bull-riding stunt as one of the show's most dangerous, because wild animals are unpredictable—especially 3,000-pound ones! Cowboys in authentic rodeo bull-riding competitions must hang on for 8 seconds in order for their times to qualify. A few of the *Fear Factor* contestants can be proud that they lasted almost that long before they were tossed off by the bullish beasts! *Ride 'em, cowboy!*

By the way, the fear of clowns—rodeo or otherwise—is coulrophobia.

IT'S A SAFE BET THAT MOST BULLFIGHTERS DON'T HAVE *TAUROPHOBIA*!

STRAIGHT FROM A PLAYER'S MOUTH!

AN INTERVIEW WITH A PAIR OF CONTESTANTS WHO LITERALLY BUZZED THROUGH AN ELECTRIFIED CHALLENGE!

Handcuffed together, contestants Randy and Tina had to collect four flags as they carefully maneuvered their way through a 40-foot maze of hundreds of electrically charged wires—each one packed with a jolting punch!

FEAR FACTOR: **What were you thinking when you found out the next stunt had to do with walking through a maze of electrical volts?**

RANDY: It was definitely a shock to see what we were doing next. We see this cage of electricity that we have to run through and grab flags from.

TINA: This torture contraption with wires going everywhere!

RANDY: There are no ands, ifs, or buts about it. You're going to get shocked. And it's going to hurt.

FEAR FACTOR: **Tina, you looked terrified before you were about to go.**

TINA: I really thought I was gonna cry. Randy has played with a stun gun before. I was never that stupid. His mentality was, "I'm just gonna bulldoze right through this." And I was like, "No, I'm, I'm, hooked to you. I don't want to do that. I'm not about to get shocked 500 million times if I can maybe just get shocked ten."

RANDY: I told Tina, "We're just gonna have to go through this." I said, "If somebody sees us doing that and they know that this is the time to beat because it's a huge disadvantage going first, 'cause you know what you have to do, so someone else is just gonna go, bam, go rush through it and take 'em off and go. So that's exactly what we did right from the beginning. I was like, "Don't worry about getting shocked. We're going to get shocked. It's going to hurt. We just gotta do it."

FEAR FACTOR: What did it feel like when you got shocked?

TINA: The first shock that I felt was when he grabbed the first flag. And it kinda just jarred me. I thought to myself, "Okay, this shock wasn't too bad, but it was because it kinda came from him and not me." Then we got to a point, in the middle of the maze, where there were so many wires. You just wanted to break through 'em and just burst to the other side. All of a sudden he's getting shocked. And I'm getting shocked. And then I'm touching two wires at the same time 'cause we're all tangled.

RANDY: You just felt it everywhere. It's like one of your eyeballs popping out!

TINA: I had no control over my body at that time. I couldn't get off the wires I was touching! I found myself reaching. I was grabbing a wire trying to pull myself out of the other one. I just lost all my senses. It shocks you so much that, by the time we got to the pole and you're trying to clip the flags on, you're just left shaking.

RANDY: You're shaking. The pole you clip your flags on to at the end was electrified, too, so you kept getting hit right up to the very end!

ANOTHER HORRIFYING FEAR FACTOR WORD SEARCH!

FIND THE WORDS ON THE LIST BELOW AND CIRCLE THEM!

(Hint: Some words might be backward or diagonal!)

CATAPULT	SEMI-TRUCKS
CAUTIOUSLY	SHAKE
ELIMINATION	TRAIN
EPISODE	TRANSFER
EXTREME	TUMBLER
HELMET	VALIANT
PLUNGE	WINNERS

Answers on page 76

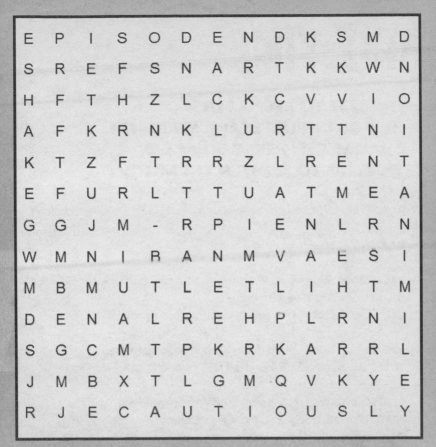

E	P	I	S	O	D	E	N	D	K	S	M	D
S	R	E	F	S	N	A	R	T	K	K	W	N
H	F	T	H	Z	L	C	K	C	V	V	I	O
A	F	K	R	N	K	L	U	R	T	T	N	I
K	T	Z	F	T	R	R	Z	L	R	E	N	T
E	F	U	R	L	T	T	U	A	T	M	E	A
G	G	J	M	-	R	P	I	E	N	L	R	N
W	M	N	I	R	A	N	M	V	A	E	S	I
M	B	M	U	T	L	E	T	L	I	H	T	M
D	E	N	A	L	R	E	H	P	L	R	N	I
S	G	C	M	T	P	K	R	K	A	R	R	L
J	M	B	X	T	L	G	M	Q	V	K	Y	E
R	J	E	C	A	U	T	I	O	U	S	L	Y

JOKE TIME!

IT'S BEST TO KEEP A SENSE OF HUMOR DURING SCARY, STRESSFUL CHALLENGES! HERE'S SOME RIB TICKLERS TO LIGHTEN THE MOOD

REPORTER: Is it true you drove your motorcycle off a cliff and didn't get hurt?
DAREDEVIL: Nah. It was just a bluff!

SALESMAN: Try this new swimsuit! You can swim, water-ski, surf, snorkel, or scuba dive with it on.
GUY: That's great! I can't do any of those things now!

JOE: I'll stop being scared if you'll stop being frightened!
SUE: That sounds like a *fear* deal!

DOCTOR: You're pretty banged up! What happened?
PATIENT: Well, Doc, I used to be a rock climber.
DOCTOR: Really? When did you give it up?
PATIENT: About halfway down.

THERE'S NO BUSINESS LIKE SCARY, PULSE-RACING SHOW BUSINESS!

By now, you might be wondering why we haven't discussed the celebrity editions of *Fear Factor* in this book. Unfortunately, contractual obligations prevent us from talking about who were in those excellent episodes, even if those cool stars themselves wouldn't mind our doing so. But we can still talk about the stunts they starred in! So, here are a few of the scariest! If you watched the episodes these stunts were featured in, you might fondly remember the exploits of certain celebrities. If you haven't seen the episodes yet, just imagine some of your favorite music, modeling, TV, or movie stars doing this stuff!

The Frozen Lake

How low can you go? Players were led to a huge, outdoor tank. The tank was filled with icy cold water and covered with Plexiglas. The idea of the stunt was to create a setting that would feel like being trapped under a frozen lake or icy surface! A small hole on top of the tank was the only entry and exit point. Each layer below was also separated by a clear, sturdy material and had only a small hole that you could get in and out of. The contestants had to dive into the freezing water and try to gather glowsticks at each level. The easily accessible red glowsticks were worth 10 points each, while the green glowsticks at the bottom level were worth 100 points each. The player with the most points would win.

YIKES-O-METER RATING: ★★★★★

Bus Surfing

While balancing on top of a double-decker bus, celebrities had to collect small flags anchored alongside the roof of the bus. Sound easy? Well, that wasn't all of it. The whole time, the bus swerved madly back and forth, in and out of the "New York" streets of a Hollywood set. One male TV star and one female star from the same show would be eliminated based on who collected the most flags!

YIKES-O-METER RATING: ★★★

Big Foot

You know those movie scenes where you see somebody stuck in a car on a train track, and the car won't start? They're trying and trying to get it going, and in the background, you hear the train approaching faster and faster? Beads of sweat are running down the driver's face—totally panicked. Well, instead of a train, picture a huge monster truck barreling down on you! In this horrifying stunt, a dozen junkyard cars were lined up side by side. At the end of the line was one *Fear Factor* car. In the car was a key ring containing six keys. Each celebrity had to find the key that started the ignition and drive the car a short distance across a finish line. The two stars with the worst times would be eliminated. But of course there was a catch. While the player fumbled with keys and stressed over their time, a 10,000 pound monster truck known as Big Foot would be making its way *on top* of the line of cars toward the *Fear Factor* car. In fact, Big Foot would crush the *Fear Factor* car—with the player inside—

if the celebrity did not move the car in time! *Put the pedal to the metal and step on it!*

YIKES-O-METER RATING: ★★★★

Floor Drop

Location: a huge dam and reservoir. Stunt props: Suspended 200 feet over the dam was a 10' x 10' Plexiglas cube. Several *Fear Factor* flags were stuck vertically along one corner of the cube. *Goal:* Each celebrity had 30 seconds to transfer the flags, one by one, to the opposite corner of the cube. *Extra twist.* After 30 seconds the bottom dropped out of the box, and the stars plummeted down toward the reservoir below! *Result:* We got to see some celebs break a sweat! Luckily, each player was attached to a bungee cord!

YIKES-O-METER RATING: ★★★★

Desert Truck Challenge

Is that a desert oasis I see, or a scared celebrity dripping in sweat? Under the bright desert sun, amid the dry scrub and desolate landscape, celebrity contestants learned what they'd have to do to claim the $50,000 prize. (All of the celebrities who appear on *Fear Factor* donate their prizes to charity.) A swerving tanker truck screeched to a halt, and the stunt was explained—the players had to stand on top of the tanker, near the rear, while it swerved down the highway at speeds of more than 40 miles per hour!

YIKES-O-METER RATING: ★★★

Platform Tilt

Star-power girls who can hold their own! In an all-female celebrity episode, the contestants had to transfer flags on a platform, from one end to the other, while the platform tilted vertically. Once the angle of the platform became too steep, the players slid off into the cold water far below, stopping the clock. The four women who transferred the most flags in the least amount of time and, of course, held their ground on the moving platform, would advance to the next round. The other two would be eliminated.

YIKES-O-METER RATING: ★★★

Caged Fear

In this stunt, each celebrity challenger would cling to a large cage suspended under a high-flying helicopter. As the helicopter whipped its way around the lake, each player had to navigate around the *outside* of the cage, which was made from cargo netting. *Fear Factor* flags were positioned in various spots around the cage, and the celebs would have to release as many flags as possible before they fell into the chilly water below. It didn't help that there were also strong, gusty winds that blew around the players as they clung to the cages.

YIKES-O-METER RATING: ★★★★

FLIP INTO THIS TRIVIA QUIZ ABOUT
EXTREME SPORTS!

Q: In the sport of rock climbing, what is the name of the spring-loaded ring that holds the rope?
a. carburetor
b. carbon
c. carabiner
d. carton

Answer: c, Most are made from aluminum, because it's a sturdy, light metal.

Q: What is the name of the bull that knocked off more than 300 riders, between 1980 and 1988, at rodeos all over the U.S.?
a. Red Rock
b. Red Bull
c. Big Red
d. Red Rider

Answer: a, That bull saw red, and the riders landed hard as a rock!

Q: American Matt Hoffman jumped off a 3,500 foot Norwegian cliff riding what?
a. his motorcycle
b. his bicycle
c. his car
d. his lawn mower

Answer: b, But he wore a parachute so he wouldn't pop his tires!

Q: In 1997, Germany's Jochen Schweizer made the world's longest bungee jump of 3,320 feet off of what?
a. a helicopter
b. an airplane
c. a bridge
d. a cliff

Answer: a, That's a loooong way down!

ThE PhOBiC Facts FiLE

HYDROPHOBIA IS
THE FEAR OF WATER!

Have you ever been swimming out in the ocean and a huge wave wiped you out and dragged you back into shore? (And then, to save face, you had to pretend like "Yeah, I was just riding that wave in!") Water is a powerful force and can instill fear in lots of people. Legend has it that sailors used to put a tattoo of a rooster on one foot and a pig on the other to prevent drowning. There's no record of whether it worked or not, but one thing is for certain—the best way to prevent drowning is to learn how to swim and always wear your life preserver while boating, water-skiing, or white-water rafting—especially if you're a contestant on *Fear Factor*!

By the way, hydrophobia is also the name for rabies, because rabies victims often have a fear of drinking water!

A PERSON CAN DROWN BUT NOT DIE—IT ALL DEPENDS ON HOW SOON THE WATER CAN BE REMOVED FROM THE LUNGS!

- White-water rafting involves riding rubber rafts down sometimes dangerous, rock-strewn, rapidly moving rivers, making it a scary but popular sport. *Sounds like a bumpy ride—but a perfect* Fear Factor *ride!*

- White-water rafts range from 6 to 12 feet long and carry four to ten paddlers. *Can't we just take a boat?*

- White-water river courses are classified on a scale of 1 to 6, with 6 being extremely dangerous and considered impossible to navigate. *Bathtubs are considered minus 2!*

- An "eddy" is a current of water running contrary to the main current, which sometimes creates a small whirlpool that rafters must avoid for safety's sake. *That's a negative spin!*

- A "sleeper" is a dangerous rock or boulder just below the surface, usually marked by little or no disturbance of the water's surface. *Better avoid these, or you could be sleeping with the fishes!*

- "Throw Bags" are small bags containing about 60 feet of rope used to rescue rafters. *Yeah, the ones who've taken an "involuntary swim"!*

- A "take out" is the point at which a rafting trip ends and the rafts and wet passengers are removed from the river. *Unless it's a* Fear Factor *"take out," which could mean that the wet passengers have just been dropped from a helicopter or submerged in a water tank with snakes and lizards!*

THE LAST CHANCE CROSSWORD!

FILL IN THE BLANKS AND SOLVE THIS HEART-POUNDING PUZZLE:

ACROSS

3. Bodies of water that many *Fear Factor* stunts take place over; rhymes with "cakes."

5. You must have this quality to play *Fear Factor*; with it, you take action, even though you might be afraid.

8. Extreme fear; rhymes with "error."

9. An exciting feeling *Fear Factor* contestants get; rhymes with "chill."

11. What a person feels while playing or watching *Fear Factor*; rhymes with "invite tent."

12. Sound an explosion makes; rhymes with "zoom."

13. Players wear this so that when they fall, they don't hit the ground; it has straps and buckles and rope attached to the players.

14. When contestants lose on *Fear Factor*, they must travel this path; rhymes with "hawk dove tame." (three words)

DOWN

1. To open a door with a key.

2. Person who does a lot of crazy, and possibly dangerous, stunts; rhymes with "scare level."

4. The force of nature that makes us fall down.

6. A frightening ride at an amusement park; it runs on a track. (two words)

7. Things you aim at.

10. When something is so scary, the follicles on your head stand up, we call it this; rhymes with "bear-grazing." (hyphenated word)

Answers on page 77

✔ ASKED & ANSWERED!

WE ASKED PLAYERS: DID YOU HAVE ANY PHOBIAS GOING INTO THE COMPETITION?

✔ "I wouldn't call them phobias but I am really afraid of spiders and really afraid of drowning, and so I hit the two big ones on the show!"

✔ "Yes, all of them, but most of all, I was afraid of my hair looking bad and my chest hair growing out."

✔ "Maybe drowning . . . and I don't like alligators!"

✔ "Give us stunts up in the air, drop us off buildings, anything physical and we knew we could accomplish it. However, the idea of eating anything that we had to catch was a whole new concept that we didn't want to endure!"

✔ "Yeah. I'm scared of being burnt to death."

✔ "Yes, I can't stand heights. Two of the three stunts happened to involve heights."

✔ "No. I had no fears going into this."

✔ "Yes, getting beat. I hate to lose."

✔ "Not really. Again, the water challenges are the hardest, just being I don't really enjoy swimming, even recreationally. If it is for my pole-vault training, I'll do it, and if it is for $50,000, I'll also do it!"

AWESOME QUOTES FROM FAMOUS PEOPLE— PAST AND PRESENT!

"If winning isn't everything, why do they keep score?"
—Vince Lombardi

"I was dreading winning. I didn't even plan a speech. I was worried that I would slip up or do something horrible. I was shaking in my seat, putting on a posed smile. Inside, I was petrified."
—Leonardo DiCaprio

"There is nothing to winning, really. That is, if you happen to be blessed with a keen eye, an agile mind, and no scruples whatsoever."
—Alfred Hitchcock

"Whoever is winning at the moment will always seem to be invincible."
—George Orwell

"Winning may not be everything, but losing has little to recommend it."
—Dianne Feinstein

"The key to winning is poise under stress."
—Paul Brown

"Winning isn't everything. Wanting to win is."
—Catfish Hunter

"Let's try winning and see what it feels like. If we don't like it, we can go back to our traditions."
—Paul Tsongas

"Losing feels worse than winning feels good."
—Vin Scully

"I do not think that winning is the most important thing. I think winning is the only thing."
—Bill Veeck

"We all have great inner power. The power is self-faith. There's really an attitude to winning. You have to see yourself winning before you win. And you have to be hungry. You have to want to conquer."
—Arnold Schwarzenegger

"I disagree with people who think you learn more from getting beat up than you do from winning."
—Tom Cruise

"Winning breeds confidence and confidence breeds winning."
—Hubert Green

By the way, fear of famous people is known as celebrity phobia.

ThE PhObiC Facts FiLe

CATAPEDAPHOBIA IS THE FEAR OF JUMPING FROM HIGH—AND LOW—PLACES!

The first successful parachute jump from a moving airplane was made by a certain Captain Berry over St. Louis, Missouri, in 1912. Note we said a "successful" jump. There were many failures before that! It takes a lot of courage to leap from a plane, or off a mountain cliff, or from a helicopter on *Fear Factor*—things a catapedaphobe could never do!

By the way, the fear of precipices is cremnophobia.

WATCH OUT! AIM YOUR JUMPS CAREFULLY!

AN INTERVIEW WITH *FEAR FACTOR'S* FIRST MILLION-DOLLAR WINNER: DURANT

He had to cross monkey bars that were suspended between helicopters, bob for pig parts in ostrich-egg yolk, transfer flags on a platform that swung like a pendulum a hundred feet off the ground, and swim through rotting fish guts. And as if that weren't enough, he had to drive a quad ATV off a cliff—and land on target—to defeat Grant, his last remaining competitor. But it was all worth it!

FEAR FACTOR: What would you say is your biggest fear?

DURANT: My biggest fear is heights, and if you saw the third stunt, "Pendulum of Death," it's obvious that I was horrified! I would grab a flag and hold on for dear life, literally! I honestly felt like a cat that did not want a bath.

FEAR FACTOR: For the first stunt you were up against eleven competitors. Were you nervous about being eliminated on that first day?

DURANT: I think everyone's biggest fear was being eliminated on the first stunt. I really wanted a chance to compete in all the stunts.

FEAR FACTOR: Do you think your physical strength gave you an advantage over some of the others?

DURANT: Absolutely not. Everyone was in great shape, and the stunts lacked any gender advantage.

FEAR FACTOR: Was there anyone in particular you were happy to see get eliminated?

DURANT: No. I actually felt bad for the others as they were eliminated. I didn't have a chance to get to know the first six that were eliminated. Then, later, we all had really bonded and it was sad to see friends go.

FEAR FACTOR: Was the first stunt, "Extreme Monkey Bars," harder than it looked?

DURANT: Not for me. I was literally in a zone for the first stunt. Also, God blessed me with long arms, and I finally understand why. As a child, I was good on the monkey bars. I guess it was like riding a bike . . . you never forget.

FEAR FACTOR: What was the most difficult part about the "Platform Swing" stunt?

DURANT: Uhh . . . I don't know, maybe being *100 feet off the ground!* Maybe the gusting wind. Maybe it was being suspended on a piece of see-through plastic in my socks as I'm being vertically swung back and forth! Oh, and grabbing flags from one edge, placing them on the other. Can I just say . . . *SCARIEST THING IMAGINABLE!*

FEAR FACTOR: Once the "Quad Launch" stunt was revealed, how did you think you'd do?

DURANT: I was always a daredevil as a kid. For me, it was a childhood fantasy come true. I was Evel Knievel all over again. I knew if I was meant to win, I would.

FEAR FACTOR: Do you think it was helpful for you to go first?

DURANT: Not really. I thought if I went first I would be there . . . to see where Grant's quad landed.

FEAR FACTOR: Once you saw Grant's landing, what were you thinking?

DURANT: Well, it was great. After I saw my landing I knew my quad didn't go very far. To watch Grant's quad hit the ground and remain motionless was truly amazing. But I needed to hear a final measurement before I could begin to rejoice.

FEAR FACTOR: Besides becoming a millionaire, what was the best part about your *Fear Factor* experience?

DURANT: I had a chance to meet eleven wonderful people from all over the nation. Actually seeing how Hollywood reality works was very interesting. Competing, competing, competing! But the million dollars doesn't hurt.

FEAR FACTOR: Are you still in shock? Any big plans for the money?

DURANT: Right now I'm back to working my two jobs and teaching in children's church. I will probably be in shock when I receive my check. I will buy a home for my family and invest wisely.

- The first designated "Hard Hat Area" in America was set up at the construction site of San Francisco's Golden Gate Bridge to protect workers from falling nails, fasteners, and other construction materials. *The guy who invented hard hats could never have imagined they'd be used for* Fear Factor *gravity-defying stunts!*

- In the 1930s, hard hats were made of aluminum, which is lightweight and durable but is a great conductor of electricity. *Today's thermoplastic hard hats are much less dangerous! You sure wouldn't want to be wearing one of those aluminum hats if you had to go through* Fear Factor*'s maze of shocks!*

- In 1938, protective baseball helmets were first worn by batters, and batting helmets were not required in the American League until 1958. *Batter up!*

- Bicyclists started wearing pith helmets (helmets with a spongy inner protective lining, and a rim to help block the sun) in the 1880s to prevent head injuries due to the design of their bicycles. (The large front wheel and smaller back wheel of bicycles caused riders to be high off the ground.) *The bigger the wheel, the harder you fall!*

- The most efficient and safe shape for a helmet in a crash resembles a bowling ball, because round, smooth surfaces slide well and avoid the tendency for the helmet to snag and jerk the wearer's neck. *The elongated shape of today's helmets is a fashion trend. Ooh la la!*

HOW ABOUT ONE MORE *FEAR FACTOR* WORD SEARCH?

FIND THE WORDS ON THE LIST BELOW AND CIRCLE THEM!

(Hint: Some words might be backward or diagonal!)

CABLES	RUSHING
ENGINE	SCARY
HANGING	SUBMARINE
IMPACT	SWINGING
QUICKLY	TEETER
RODEO	TRAPPED
ROOFTOP	WHEEL

Answers on page 78

P	Z	L	F	H	A	N	G	I	N	G
J	R	O	D	E	O	N	I	K	T	R
E	R	F	W	R	I	E	M	R	Y	Y
K	N	T	M	G	T	N	P	O	R	L
W	P	I	N	T	C	I	A	O	A	K
Z	K	I	G	A	R	R	C	F	C	G
Y	W	L	D	N	L	A	T	T	S	I
S	F	L	M	E	E	M	P	O	D	U
R	E	T	E	E	T	B	P	P	R	Q
S	N	H	Y	C	B	U	C	C	E	K
N	W	G	N	I	H	S	U	R	L	D

TRIVIA QUIZ!

**ANSWER THESE STUNT-RELATED
QUESTIONS AND SEE HOW YOU RATE.**

Q: What was the very first stunt on the
very first episode of *Fear Factor*?
 a. jumping from one blimp to another
 b. leaping through a ring of fire
 c. being dragged by horses
 d. catapulting over the HOLLYWOOD sign

Answer: c, What a drag!

Q: In one stunt, players hung from bungee cords
and shot at a target with what?
 a. slingshots
 b. paint ball guns
 c. pea shooters
 d. rubber bands

Answer: b, A colorful challenge!

Q: At Irwindale Speedway, challengers tried to stop
on a dime using what kind of vehicles?
 a. go-carts
 b. market baskets
 c. Formula One racers
 d. tricycles

Answer: a, Putta-putt-putt, zoom!

Q: During the Flag Snag stunt, players had to shinny out on a pole suspended over ten stories in the air at what location?

a. Las Vegas

b. oil refinery

c. Times Square, New York City

d. baseball stadium

Answer: b. And you just know they were hoping their hands didn't get oily!

Q: In the Save Your Spouse challenge, contestants had to rescue their spouses from what?

a. path of a monster truck

b. speeding roller coaster

c. flaming car

d. underwater box

Answer: d. Saved from bubbly trouble on the double!

Q: Players had to ride what, as if it were a bucking bronco, in the Helicopter Rodeo stunt?

a. barrel

b. raft

c. landing skid

d. log

Answer: a. Hope it wasn't as painful as it looked!

Q: The Ferris Wheel challenge had contestants running on the top of a spinning wheel and included what extra element of danger?

a. rain

b. mud

c. snow

d. fire

Answer: c. But in Los Angeles? That's really scary!

Q: During the stunt in which contestants had to drive a car into a pool, the time clock would stop after they placed their *Fear Factor* flag where?

a. beach ball
b. beach towel
c. pool ladder
d. cabana

Answer: c, What better way to climb to success?

Q: During one Christmas episode, players rode on a sled 100 feet in the air to collect what holiday items?

a. candy canes
b. figgy puddings
c. colored lights
d. ornament bulbs

Answer: a, What a sweet game!

Q: Players slid down the side of a pyramid during a *Fear Factor* episode that was filmed where?

a. Mexico City
b. Pyramid Lake
c. Egypt
d. Las Vegas

Answer: d, Talk about gambling with their lives!

Q: Which of these locations has been used as a *Fear Factor* stunt site?

a. deserted factory
b. deserted highway
c. deserted airplane landing strip
d. deserted rock quarry

Answer: Trick question! All answers are correct!

(To see how you scored, check on the next page!)

SO, HOW DID YOU DO?

COUNT THE NUMBER OF QUESTIONS YOU GOT RIGHT, AND SEE WHERE YOU RATE ON THE *FEAR FACTOR* EXPERT YIKES-O-METER!

0-2 Correct = YIKES-O-METER EXPERT RATING ★
You're a *Fear Factor* newbie; you recently discovered the show, or else you hide your eyes during the scary, dangerous parts!

3-5 Correct = YIKES-O-METER EXPERT RATING ★★
You're a *Fear Factor* rookie; you are stunt knowledgeable, but you'd probably still scream if your bike lost its front tire while doing a wheelie!

6-8 Correct = YIKES-O-METER EXPERT RATING ★★★
You're a *Fear Factor* semipro; you'll jump ramps, grind rails, and hang ten, but you still get dizzy if you look straight down from a third-story window!

9-10 Correct = YIKES-O-METER EXPERT RATING ★★★★
You're a *Fear Factor* pro; your mom fears the day you buy your first motorcycle!

11 Correct = YIKES-O-METER EXPERT RATING ★★★★★
You're a *Fear Factor* all-star; no one will be surprised when you end up on TV after parachuting from a cliff in Brazil. More importantly . . .

FEAR IS NOT A FACTOR FOR YOU!

ANSWERS

TO CROSSWORD PUZZLE ON PAGE 7:

SOLUTION

TO MAZE PUZZLE ON PAGE 11:

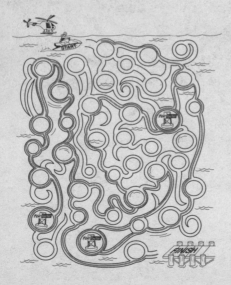

ANSWERS

TO WORD MATCH ON PAGE 13:

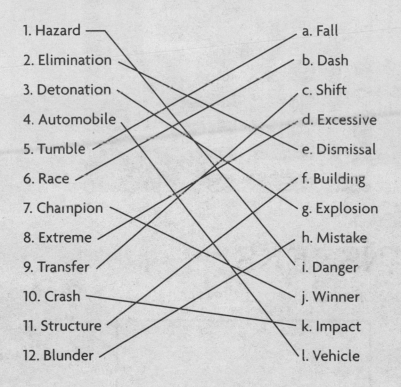

1. Hazard
2. Elimination
3. Detonation
4. Automobile
5. Tumble
6. Race
7. Champion
8. Extreme
9. Transfer
10. Crash
11. Structure
12. Blunder

a. Fall
b. Dash
c. Shift
d. Excessive
e. Dismissal
f. Building
g. Explosion
h. Mistake
i. Danger
j. Winner
k. Impact
l. Vehicle

ANSWERS

TO CROSSWORD PUZZLE ON PAGE 17:

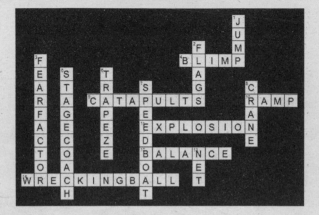

ANSWERS

TO WORD SEARCH PUZZLE ON PAGE 25:

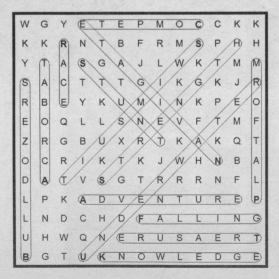

ANSWERS

TO WORD MATCH ON PAGE 30:

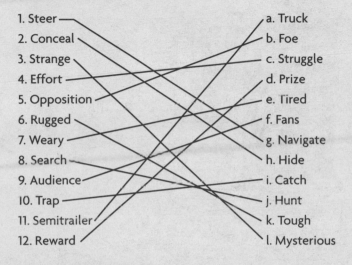

1. Steer
2. Conceal
3. Strange
4. Effort
5. Opposition
6. Rugged
7. Weary
8. Search
9. Audience
10. Trap
11. Semitrailer
12. Reward

a. Truck
b. Foe
c. Struggle
d. Prize
e. Tired
f. Fans
g. Navigate
h. Hide
i. Catch
j. Hunt
k. Tough
l. Mysterious

ANSWERS

TO CROSSWORD PUZZLE ON PAGE 35:

SOLUTION

TO MAZE PUZZLE ON PAGE 41:

ANSWERS

TO WORD SEARCH PUZZLE ON PAGE 47:

ANSWERS

TO CROSSWORD PUZZLE ON PAGE 57:

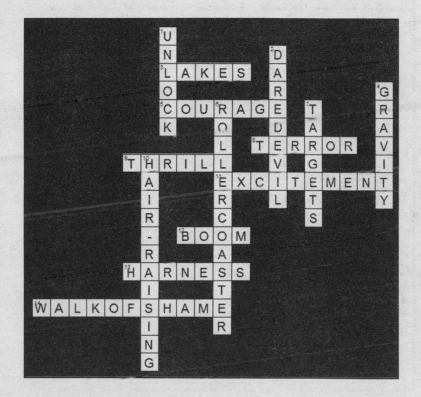

ANSWERS

TO WORD SEARCH PUZZLE ON PAGE 67:

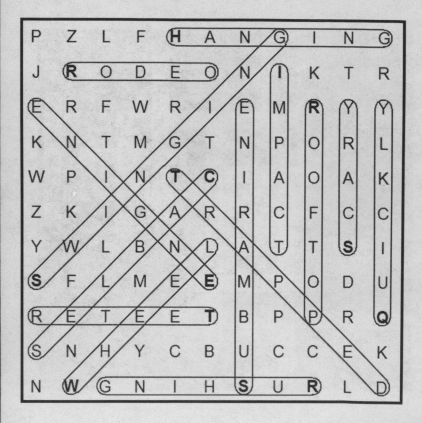

ABOUT THE AUTHOR

Jesse Leon McCann is a top-ten *New York Times* bestselling author. He lives in a suburb of Los Angeles with his busy comic-book-store-owning wife, two active children, and four frisky felines. With all that traffic around, you can bet the fear of fumbling, bumbling, tumbling, slipping, tripping, flipping, and falling is a factor for him!

HELI-PLATFORM ESCAPE

For the heli-platform escape stunt, these female contestants found themselves taking the ride of their lives. The women soared through the air while shackled to a dangling platform.

Too bad they had to be chained down; they probably missed a great view!

The contestants had to free themselves as quickly as possible and then take a plunge into a freezing-cold lake.

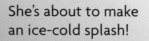

She's about to make
an ice-cold splash!

That's gonna be one
painful plunge!

DUAL HELI-DISK

For the dual heli-disk stunt, the sibling contestant pairs were handcuffed to a platform swinging beneath a helicopter. The keys to free them were attached to a rope beneath the platform. Once freed, they had to plunge into the water below.

It's a family affair. These Las Vegas sisters look pretty happy before the stunt begins. . . .

But once they're in midair, the fear factor starts kicking in.

Fear factor

Brothers Chip and Kelly look determined to get off that platform. But first they have to get that key.

These brothers have matching Sanskrit tattoos that translate to "Family Strength." Guess the tattoos don't lie—they won the stunt, finishing with an amazing time of 47.9 seconds.

SEPARATING PLATFORM TRANSFER

For this stunt, competing couples had to jump from platform to platform, high above the ground. The platforms slowly separated while the couples jumped back and forth, transferring flags from side to side.

This stunt looks easy as pie at first. . . .

But as the clock keeps ticking, the fear factor starts to rise. Talk about taking a leap of faith!

Good thing they're wearing harnesses!

WATER PADDLE

Remember going swimming when you were little and getting dunked by the big kids? This stunt is sort of like that. Except the water is freezing, and the players are strapped to a partially submerged spinning wheel. While holding their breath underwater, they have to find the correct keys to free them.

This contestant tries out the nose-plugging technique. Seems like it might be harder to grab a key if you're only using one hand though!

SUSPENDED LOGROLLING

Logrolling, also called birking, is a real sport, but it is usually done on a log floating in water. *Fear Factor*-style logrolling is done on a giant rotating cylinder floating in the air. Those with a fear of heights should NOT attempt this death-defying stunt.

According to a logrolling source, rule number one is: Don't look at your feet!

Oops! Looks like someone should have told this player that information sooner.